The Hole
In The
Wall Gang

Maureen Spurgeon

CARNIVAL

"All right, Egon!" cried Ray Stantz, as The Ghostbusters speeded along in their Ectomobile. "What's the job, this time?"

"Cheese!"

"Cheese?"

"Limburger cheese! Charles Von Limburger is the heir to the world's largest cheese fortune! He's also been landed with a haunted mansion . . ."

"A haunted mansion?" Somehow, thought Peter Venkman, it all sounded just a bit corny. "Well – at least, we know . . ."

But, even he had to admit that the place looked the part, with spires and towers and domes casting black shadows all around the stormy landscape. Even the front door opened with a series of tooth-griding creaks and groans.

"Yes?"

Ray had to look twice before he saw the tiny man standing in front of him.

"Oh – er, hi! We're The Ghostbusters!"

"Oh, yes!" The man certainly seemed pleased to see them and showed them inside. "Come right in! I'm Charles Von Limburger! And this," he went on, extending a hand towards a woman who seemed to tower above him, "is Lady Limburger!"

Egon wondered if they ought to shake hands, but Von Limburger was already leading the way into a huge room. Dark and mysterious shadows hovered all around.

"We moved here three weeks ago," Limburger was saying, "and we've been experiencing strange supernatural manifestations ever since!"

"Crashing and banging," added his wife, "howlings and moanings, and the most frightful gruntings and things falling out of cupboards . . ."

The Ghostbusters glanced at each other. It seemed like they'd heard it all before.

"We-we've seen them lurking in the dark," Limburger continued in a frightened whisper. "Huge, red-eyed monsters, with scrabbling claws . . ."

"Moaning and scratching at the walls," Lady Limburger chimed in.

"Rustling in the shadows, and wailing in the dungeons . . ."

"Psycho Kinetic Energy readings indicate that the source of the trouble is upstairs!" interrupted Egon, consulting his PKE meter.

"Well," said Limburger, "goodbye, then!"

"We've decided to leave the house for the week-end," Lady Limburger explained. "So as to give you a chance to do your job without us being in the way!"

They had grabbed their luggage and disappeared, even before a fast-talking Ghostbuster like Peter Venkman could think of anything to say.

"Right!" said Egon, breaking the stunned
silence. "Let's get to work!"

"I was afraid you'd say that!" groaned
Winston – but he began following Egon up the
wide Limburger staircase all the same, humping
Proton Packs, PKE meters and ghost traps,
along with Peter and Ray.

"Okay," he whispered, as a door at the end of
the corridor loomed towards them. "This is the
last chance for anyone to have a bad feeling!"

Egon pushed the door open, and The
Ghostbusters found themselves looking into a
huge bedroom, the furniture covered in white
sheets.

"It's in here!" Egon nodded slowly, pointing a
finger towards a wall. "This is it . . .!"

"A hole in the wall?" gasped Ray in stunned
disbelief. "You must be kidding, Egon! Hello?"
he shouted putting his face in the hole. "Come

out, come out, wherever you are . . ."

And nobody was more surprised than Ray when something *did* come out! Sixty pounds of slime, to be precise, hitting his face at forty miles an hour!

"Oh, boy!" Peter grinned. "I must be the lucky one, today! I'm usually the one who gets slimed."

Poor old Peter! He spoke too soon. The next moment a great mass of slime came shooting out of the hole and hit him on the back of the neck!

"Well," he said, turning around, "at least it didn't hit me in the face!"

Splat! Being slimed twice on one job was enough to make any self-respecting Ghostbuster reach for his Proton Pack.

"Okay!" Peter yelled, firing his Proton Gun. "Eat purple death, cold slime!"

"Peter," said Egon warningly, "that may not be such a good idea . . ."

But a bright purple proton beam had already streaked into the hole, crackling and fizzing and sparkling like it was Guy Fawkes Night.

Everything went quiet.

"Is that it?" asked Ray, somewhat disbelievingly. No job had ever been so easy! Maybe, Egon thought, Peter had done right, after all . . .

Only Winston saw a tiny ghost crawling out of the hole and land on the floor, only seconds before a rumble sounded from the other side . . .

"Aaaaagh – !"

"Yeeek – !"

"No-o-o-o-ooo!"

What else could The Ghostbusters say, with plaster falling, walls cracking, paintings sliding down from walls, and furniture toppling over?

Whilst all the time, the rumbling grew louder and louder, making the whole house shake, causing smaller holes to appear all over the place!

"Listen!" Ray yelled at last, pointing a finger. "It's coming right at us! Look!"

They all looked. It was just about the fiercest, ugliest, nastiest ghost any of them had seen in a long, long time . . . all six inches of it!

And yet, that mini ghost seemed to be an absolute whizz at dodging the beams from Peter's Proton Gun. Again and again he fired. And, again and again, that nasty little spook escaped. And each time Peter fired and missed he smashed another hole in the wall. Until, at last – zap! Their ghost trap opened with a deadly glow, and all was quiet.

But, once the smoke from Winston's gun had cleared, that was when The Ghostbusters saw the full extent of the damage . . . Holes in the walls, the floor, the ceiling . . .

And, as if that weren't enough, tiny little ghosts began coming out of every single one,

until The Ghostbusters could hardly move. Mini ghosts were sitting on the equipment, riding on their shoes and Proton Packs – they were everywhere they looked!

"There's something horrible in that hole!" pronounced Egon. Even one little ghost was shuddering in fear. "I must send in a probe!"

Lucky The Ghostbusters had a no-nonsense guy like Winston in the team. He soon set about widening the hole with his bare hands, whilst Egon brought in a mini-helicopter, ready for Ray to fix on a remote control unit and TV camera.

"Okay, Egon," said Ray at last, unwinding a huge coil of cable. "Whenever you're ready!"

"Careful with those cables, Ray," Egon warned, working the controls to send the mini helicopter up in the air, then into the hole.

"No problem!" Ray grinned cheerfully. But, he spoke too soon . . .

In one single instant, the cables were taut, then began spinning off the reel so fast that Ray only just managed to grab the end!

"Yee-oo-www-rrrgggh – !" he yelled – which is about all anyone can say when they are being yanked headlong into a hole in a wall, then out again, scattering splinters of wood, slabs of plaster, little green ghoulies – and three Ghostbusters – all over the place.

"What did you see, Ray?" demanded Winston, once they'd all got their breath back. "And what happened to your hair?"

"I saw the supernatural world . . ." Ray's voice sounded supernatural, too. "The Outer Limits . . . The Twilight Zone . . ."

"Come on guys," Egon interrupted. "We'd best inspect the damage!"

Walls blown out . . . Wreckage everywhere . . . There was hardly anything left worth inspecting. Not unless you counted holes. Millions and trillions of holes, all with little green ghosties piling out.

The only thing Winston could find intact was one small piece of wood panelling. And even that had a knot hole in it, with a green mini ghost squirting through.

And when he tried shaking the green ghost off, still more tiny ghosts came oozing out, intent on following the first one!

"Hey!" Winston was clearly enthralled. "Hey, fellas, look!"

"Of course!" cried Egon. "The size of the hole determines the size of the ghosts! The smaller the hole, the smaller the ghosts!"

"So, the bigger the hole," Ray added thoughtfully, "the bigger the ghost gets . . ."

"Wow . . ." breathed Winston. "That hole over there, it's so big, there's not much wall left for it to be a hole in!"

Egon was already turning pale. "I don't even want to think about the size of the ghost that could come through that hole!"

"I don't think you'll have time to think!" Ray Stantz yelled above the menacing tread of thundering footsteps, getting nearer every minute. "Here it comes!"

"Proton Guns at the ready!" commanded Egon. "Fire!"

Ion beams streaked out without stopping. It was only when the smoke had cleared that all four Ghostbusters realised the dreadful truth.

All they had done was to make one enormous hole even more enormous, spreading up to the ceiling, down towards the floor, and out into the next-door rooms, almost as far as the eye could see!

And – judging by the footsteps which were pounding loud enough to set the whole Limburger mansion shaking like a bowl of jelly in an earthquake – there was still worse to come!

"Egon," gulped Peter Venkman bravely. "I-I think it's time to put Plan B into operation!"

"Plan B . . .?" echoed Ray and Winston.

"Run!" bellowed Peter, already going like a champion sprinter.

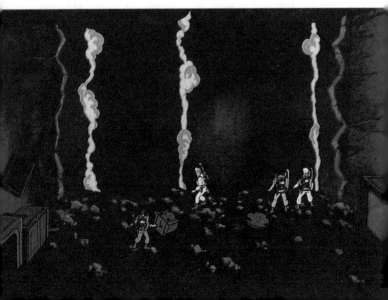

The Limburger mansion was still shaking and shuddering, quaking and quivering, when the team skidded to a breathless halt outside.

Then, suddenly, yet slowly, with a whole lot of creaking and crashing and banging, the entire mansion collapsed like a giant pack of cards.

All The Ghostbusters could see was a huge pile of rubble. Every one of the little green ghosts had disappeared. Or, so they thought . . .

"The hole is still there, under all that rubble," Egon told them, his PKE meter pointing straight down, above the smoking ruin which remained. "Only now, it's fifty feet across . . ."

"F-fifty feet?" stammered Ray Stantz.

"That means," Peter joined in, "that whatever comes out of that hole will be the biggest thing we've ever seen . . ."

His words faltered to a stop, as the ground began rumbling beneath their feet, and a gigantic, clawed hand scrabbled free!

The Ghostbusters soon saw that this was on the end of a huge, gigantic arm which reached all round as if it couldn't wait to make a grab at something.

"Can't we give it a peace offering?" suggested Peter, trying to be funny, as usual. He hardly expected Winston to start delving into his pockets!

"Hey!" he shouted. "I've still got that piece of wood panelling with the knot-hole in it!"

"Throw it away, Winston!" Ray snapped impatiently, whirling around as Egon gave an excited yell.

"Ray, you're brilliant! Throw that hole into the big hole, Winston! It's our only hope!"

By now, another hand was emerging, dust and rubble flying all around. But Winston Zeddmore didn't flinch once, not even when the gigantic head finally burst through, baring a whole mouthful of deadly-looking fangs.

"Well, well!" he heard himself saying. "Quite a big one, aren't you?"

The monster ghost roared in reply – and this was Winston's Big Chance!

He flung the piece of wood with the hole in it right down the enormous gullet, then fled for cover.

It was enough to make any monster's face curdle. The beast shrunk, shrivelled and withered all at once, fast sinking back into the hole in the ground with a last few pathetic-sounding cries.

Still the ground shook and shivered, quaked

and quivered. Then came the loudest explosion any of them had ever heard, resounding for hundreds of miles around.

But, when the Limburgers drew up in the limousine, it was clear they were none too impressed.

"Where is our house?" demanded Lady Limburger.

"It was a bigger job than we expected!" explained Peter. "We'll send you our bill in the morning!"

Ray Stantz could hear Lady Limburger raging as he took the wheel of ECTO-1.

"That's what you get for hiring a bunch of amateurs! Next time, call the REAL Ghostbusters!"

XMAS MARKS THE SPOT

Peter Venkman didn't believe in Christmas. All that snow people sang about, the cosy fires and the present-giving around the tree . . . It just wasn't his favourite time of year.

"His Dad was always away on business at Christmas," Ray told Egon and Winston. "That affects a kid after a while!"

Well, anyway, it was Peter who took things like jobs on Christmas Eve in his stride. Even if that meant trying to find a telephone when the Ectomobile broke down at the foot of a snow-covered hill. A hill which – suddenly – seemed a whole lot steeper than it looked.

Suddenly, the whole landscape began shimmering, like a strange mirage on the desert sand, flashing on and off, on and off.

It was sharp-eyed Winston who noticed the

gas-lamps first, glowing yellow through a break
in the snow, shining down on cobbled streets,
on sloping roofs and attic windows.

"Wow . . ." breathed Ray, hardly able to
believe his eyes. "This place is ancient, like
something out of Victorian England!"

"Too old for a telephone?" argued Peter. "You
wait and see!"

Heads bent against the bitterly cold wind, The
Ghostbusters barely heard the hansom cabs
rumbling along, paid little attention to the
gentlemen in frocked coats and top hats
nodding to one another as they passed a group

of lantern-lit carol-singers . . .

How about that butcher's shop in the distance, Peter wondered, the one where a kind-faced man and his crippled son were carrying a small goose out into the frosty night? Would there be a telephone there that they could use?

But, it was tough going. They had only gone a little way along the dimly-lit street, when an echo of the most nerve-shattering, hideous moaning seemed to make their hair stand on end.

"What the heck was that?" asked Winston.

"Sounds like it came from a house over there!" Ray shouted, pointing down a dark, narrow lane.

"Picking up strong Psycho Kinetic Energy readings from inside!" nodded Egon, looking up from his PKE meter. "Right up there!"

The words had barely left his mouth, when the ghost of a man flew out from an upstairs window, trailing chains, iron boxes and lead weights behind him as he rose into the air.

"I'm getting plenty more readings!" Egon yelled.

Sure enough, three more spooks were already zooming in towards an open window, a series of flashes coming from inside the room!

"No!" screamed a tormented voice. "Go away!

"Oh, boy," sighed Peter, reaching for his Proton Pack. "Seems a Ghostbuster's work is never done!"

All four stormed in through the front door, rushing past the big, heavy doorknocker. They paid no attention to the desperate cries of the ghost they had seen seconds before. "No! I, Jacob Marley, I tell you – leave the house of Ebeneezer Scrooge! No-o-o-o-o – !" it shrieked after them.

But The Ghostbusters were already racing through the dusty, dark, old house, Proton Guns at the ready, straight across the hall, and into the bedroom.

Then, they stopped, reeling back in surprise. There, in front of them, were three ghosts. And Scrooge.

"Well, don't just stand there!" he cackled. "Do something!"

There came a cry of despair and anguish from the ghosts. "Young Sirs, no!"

Release us! Or you and all Christmasses to come will pay the price!"

But ion beams were already streaking out into the gloom, with Egon pulling out the ghost trap from under his jacket, ready to slide across the floor.

The doors to the trap opened, then closed, the three Ghosts of Christmas safely inside. The job, it seemed, couldn't have been easier.

"You've beaten them!" cried Scrooge in delight. "Gentlemen, what you've done here tonight . . ."

"Is worth every penny!" finished Peter, writing out a bill. "If you'd like to make your cheque payable to The Ghostbusters . . ."

"Money?" screeched Scrooge in disbelief. "You charge money for this?" He scrabbled inside a battered purse and flung a gold coin at their feet. This I'll pay, and not a shilling more!"

"Hey! A half sovereign, in mint condition!" Ray's eyes gleamed. "Thanks a lot, Mr Scrooge!"

They were all glad to pile into ECTO-1. Ray flicked the ignition switch, but without much hope. Nobody was more surprised than he was when the engine purred into life without any trouble. Everyone clapped and cheered at the thought of going home.

Everyone, that is, except Egon.

"I keep thinking there's something very familiar about what happened," he kept saying, all the way back to Ghostbusters' HQ. "As if it's all happened somewhere before . . ."

"Okay if you go and unload the ghost trap in the containment unit, Egon?" asked Ray when they arrived home. "We're taking Peter to get a Christmas tree!"

"A tree?" echoed Janine, their secretary. "For Christmas? Huh!"

"But – I thought you liked Christmas, Janine,"

said Egon, puzzled.

There didn't seem to be much Christmas spirit in the streets of New York, either. Every time Winston called out: "Hi! Merry Christmas!" – back came the same answer. "Bah! Humbug!" –

And instead of garlands and fairy lights, the face of Ebeneezer Scrooge appeared everywhere – even on hundreds of books in the shop windows, all entitled "A CHRISTMAS HUMBUG, BY EBENEEZER SCROOGE".

"Scrooge?" cried Peter. "But – he's the guy we helped! So, how could we help him, unless – unless we went back in time . . ."

"Those ghosts we trapped," said Winston, "they must have been the ghosts of Christmas Past, Christmas Present, and Christmas Future!"

"Everyone knows that story!" snarled a passer-by. "In 1837, Scrooge defeated the three

Christmas ghosts, and put an end to Christmas. And good riddance!"

"We went back in time," Ray Stantz gasped in horror. "And, by changing the past – we've changed the present!"

"No problem," said Peter. "We took the ghosts, all we have to do is put them back."

"But Egon's about to unload them into the containment unit!" yelled Winston, beginning to panic. "We-we've got to stop him!"

Too late! Egon had just pulled the final switch as they raced down to the basement, drawing out the empty ghost trap with grim satisfaction.

"Scrooge's three ghosts are safely inside!" he nodded. "Okay?"

"No!" wailed Peter. "Oh, Egon, we just killed Christmas! It's gone forever, unless we can go back in time and return them to Scrooge's place!"

"I'll have to make a hairline crack in the containment grid," Egon said at last. "Then I'll go inside the unit, and if I get the ghosts, I'll see you at Scrooge's. I've got about an hour, at the very most."

"And, if you don't make it?" Winston felt he just had to know.

"Then you will have to become the three ghosts of Christmas!"

It was an action replay . . . The snow-covered streets, ECTO-1 shuddering to a halt, the three Ghostbusters climbing to the top of a hill, the glow of the gas lamps, the crooked windows, arched doorways . . .

Only this time, Scrooge was looking quite pleased with himself, sitting at a desk with a quill pen.

"A Christmas Humbug . . ." he muttered as he wrote. "By Ebeneezer Scrooge! My, I do like the

ring of that!''

"H-hello?'' he cried out, half in fear. "Wh-who is there?''

He waited, the silence seeming to cut into his very soul, like a knife. Then came a blood-curdling cry, an eerie figure in a white tunic crashed into the room and landed on top of him.

"Yaaaaggh!'' Peter wasn't really sure that this was how a Christmas ghost should sound, but he was determined to do his best.

"Wh-what are you?'' blustered Scrooge, glasses slipping down from his crooked nose. "Who do you think you are?''

"I'm Peter – '' Venkman coughed hurriedly. "I mean, I am the ghost of Christmas Past!''

"B-but, you were defeated! I saw it myself! If you are the ghost of Christmas Past, where is the glow which surrounds you?''

"Oh, yeah . . .'' Peter muttered remembering the lightning device in his costume. "Let's see, where's that switch . . .''

And for once, Peter lit up with the spirit of Christmas, gleaming and sparkling all over the place, glinting into Scrooge's beady eyes.

"And now, Scrooge,'' he said, taking out some picture-view binoculars from underneath his robe, "how about a trip down Memory Lane?''

Back at Ghostbuster's HQ, Egon was putting the finishing touches to his Master Plan.

"Okay, Janine,'' he said at last. "Hit the button!''

A beam of light flashed from a device on the

table to the containment unit, making a thin, hairline crack appear. Egon nodded, satisfied, and reached for a switch on his uniform.

"Oh, Egon!" Janine wailed in alarm. "Please – please be careful!"

Another flash of light, and Egon, now as thin and as wispy-looking as any of the ghosts, was sucked in through the crack. Janine could hardly bear it. Even Slimer seemed like great company just then.

And, at the same time as Egon found himself whirling and tumbling around looking for ghosts, Peter was whirling old Scrooge around in a wheelchair, picture-view binoculars strapped to his mean, bony old head.

"My old school!" breathed Scrooge. "I spent many a Christmas there, while my father was away. But, I had my books! What more did I need?"

"A lot more, I'd say," murmured Peter softly. "I know, I sure did. But, just because you had a rotten past, that's no reason to blame Christmas . . ." he heard his voice fading into nothing, listening to the words he had just spoken.

"I think," he said, "that's a lesson we could all stand to learn."

"Maybe," nodded Scrooge. "But, I am still not convinced!"

"Then, you've got two more chances!" Peter leapt on to the window sill and gave a tug on the rope, ready for Ray and Winston to haul him up into the air.

None of them could know that, at that same moment, Egon was swimming through the sea of white mist which enclosed every one of the ghosts which The Ghostbusters had ever captured, trying desperately to find the right ones!

"The hour's almost over!" Janine screamed over the walkie-talkie. "Come back, Egon! You'll be trapped!"

"No, wait! There they are, Janine!" She could see him waving frantically to the Christmas ghosts on the TV monitor. "Hurry!" he called out to them. "Follow me!"

The effect of his words was amazing. Whole processions of ghostly characters and creatures began scrambling towards the hairline crack which would give them their freedom.

"Get to the grid device, Janine!" Egon yelled over the radio. "If they start to come through, turn it off! Don't let them escape!"

But, time was passing – and passing fast. By now, Winston was being Christmas Present, swinging from the rope with a very green-looking Scrooge, and pointing to the darkened city below!

"See them?" he demanded. "The workhouses where you send the poor?"

"N-no, spirit!" Scrooge's teeth chattered more than he did!

"Well, hang around! We'll swing past them again in just a second!"

"Hurry up, Egon – " Peter muttered, checking his watch. "Where are the *real* Christmas ghosts?"

He had no means of knowing it – but, even as he spoke, those ghosts were right behind Egon in the containment unit!

"Keep going!" he yelled at them. "Don't look back!"

Even Slimer was exhausted. But, at last, they were free – only a split second before Egon's device exploded in a shower of sparks and flashes.

"Inside!" Egon commanded, grabbing a ghost trap. "Please! It's faster!'

In a matter of moments, ECTO-2 left HQ, with Egon at the controls – and the ghost trap safely by his side.

Things at Scrooge's were now getting desperate. So desperate, that Ray Stantz, alias Christmas Present, was having to amuse Scrooge with a game of charades. Charades, of all things!

Then, a cry from the street below made Winston dash to the window.

"Look, Peter!" he cried. "It's Egon!"

And, so it was, racing along and waving madly with one hand, and holding up the ghost trap with the other.

"I got them!" he was yelling. "I got them!"

"Nice work, Egon!" Winston shouted back, unwinding the rope at the same time. "Now, catch!"

And, if Egon crashed through the window and sent everyone flying – well, so what? All that mattered was that the three ghosts of Christmas were back where they belonged, crawling thankfully out of the ghost trap.

"Why!" Scrooge squinted painfully, seeing the mass of cables entangling Egon.

"Jacob Marley, still wearing the chains! Why have you returned?"

"To say that you will be visited this night by three spirits!"

"Three more?" Scrooge groaned. "I-I'm not sure I can stand it!"

"So much for all our hard work," said Ray. "I wonder if old Scrooge has learned his lesson?"

"Yes," came Christmas Present's voice. "I think he has."

"Just as I believe," he added, turning towards Peter, "you have learned yours."

"Yes," answered Peter, looking more serious than any of The Ghostbusters had ever seen him before. "Believe me, I have. I don't think I ever appreciated Christmas until I lost it. Now – can we go home?"

"You only had to ask!" Christmas Present gave a merry-sounding laugh, "Just take hold of my robe!"

None of The Ghostbusters ever really knew

what happened next. They only remembered a sudden, blinding flurry of sparkling white snow. When it cleared, they were back inside the old fire station, Janine and Slimer setting a bowl of punch on the table!

"How – how did we – ?" stammered Ray. "We were over at Scrooge's – "

The question is," said Winston, "did it work? Is Christmas back?"

His answer came in a chorus of Good King Wenceslas from the street – then, the sound of sleigh bells tinkling through the frosty, night air.

"Come along, Dancer and Prancer. Donner and Blitzen!" came a voice.

"No . . ." said Peter, after a pause. "It couldn't be – could it?"

Then he laughed. A happy, child's laugh of the boyhood he had never known. "Then, again – why not? Merry Christmas, everyone!"